# Hawaii is a Rainbow

Stephanie Feeney

photographs by Jeff Reese
designed by Jill Chen Loui

A Kolowalu Book
University of Hawaii Press
Honolulu

Library of Congress Catalog Card Number 85-50569
ISBN 0-8248-1007-4
Manufactured in Singapore

99 98 97 96 95 93   9 8 7 6 5 4

# About the book

Children have always loved rainbows. Rainbows appear and disappear as if by magic and they make the world appear brighter and more beautiful, but you can never touch or hold the glowing arch of colored light. In Hawaii we have lots of sunshine and light rain so many rainbows are formed as the sun's rays pass through drops of rain.

The first Hawaiians called the rainbow *ānuenue* and believed that when a rainbow appeared it was a sign that something important was about to happen. Rainbows are still a very special part of life in Hawaii. Children paint pictures of them, people write songs and poems about them, and everyone enjoys their beauty.

And Hawaii is, in some ways, like a rainbow. Many different colors are seen on the islands and they seem more vivid in the clear air and bright sunshine. Green islands ringed with sparkling white waves rise out of a turquoise ocean. The skies are brilliant blue during the day and at sunrise and sunset are often colored with shades of gold, orange, red, magenta, and purple. Plants, flowering trees, birds, shells, and tropical fish are also brightly colored.

The people of Hawaii are also like the rainbow. They come from many places in the world, have skin, hair, and eyes of different colors, speak many languages, and have different kinds of food, celebrations, and art. Like the colors of the rainbow when the people come together they seem even more beautiful.

In this book we use the colors of the rainbow—red, orange, yellow, green, blue, and purple—as a way to organize pictures of some of the people, places, plants, and animals of Hawaii. *Hawaii is a Rainbow* has been created to help children learn about colors and about Hawaii. We hope that it will help both children and adults to appreciate the rich variety and the very special beauty of our islands.

# Red

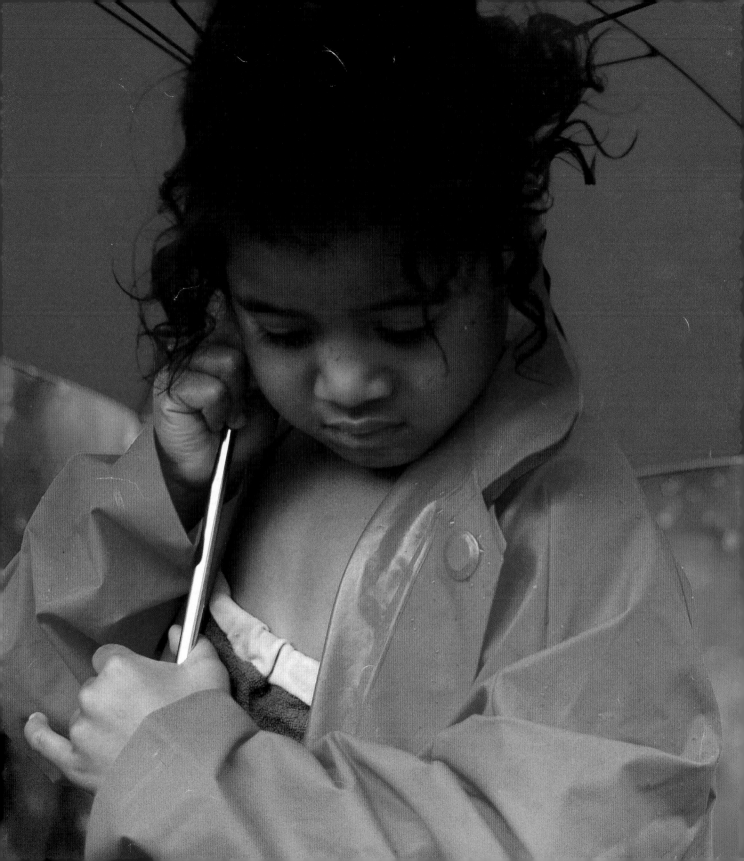

# Orange

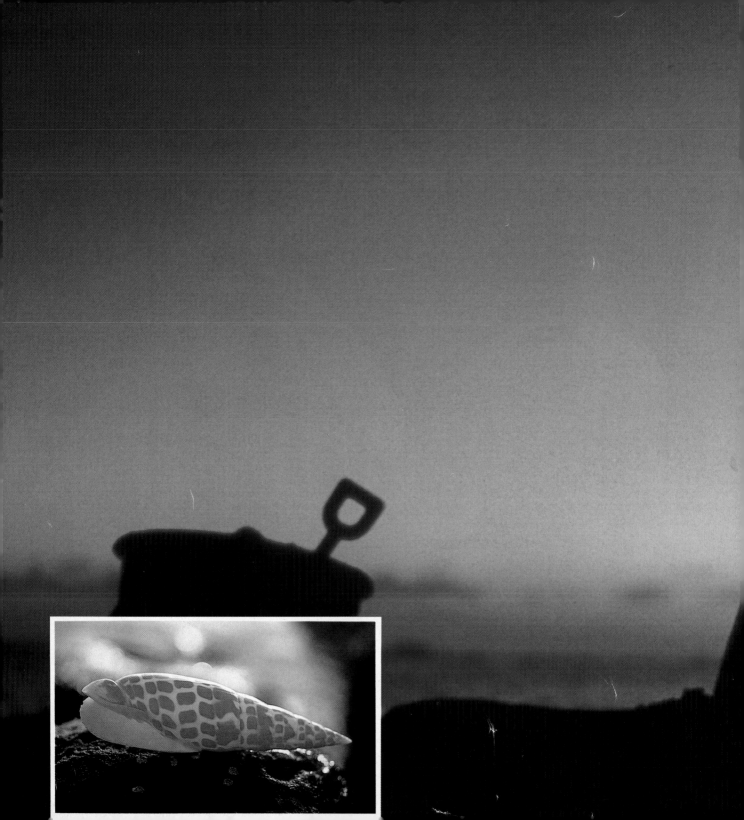

# Yellow

# Green

# Blue

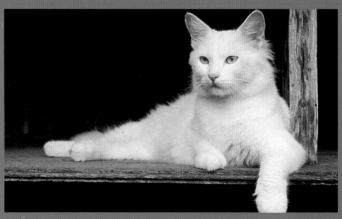

# Purple

# Sharing this book with children

Looking at a book with a special adult can be a wonderful experience for a child. It can also contribute to learning language and concepts and interest in books and reading. The pictures in *Hawaii is a Rainbow* have been selected for their appeal to young children, and the background information about Hawaii that follows provides information at the level of their understanding.

A child under the age of three will probably be most interested in the subject matter of the pictures. Look at them together, discuss what you see and your feelings and reactions. Older preschoolers and school-age children may want more information about the things in the pictures that are especially interesting to them. If the child wants to know more, refer to the sections that deal with the islands, plants and animals, and people of Hawaii.

Most young children are fascinated by color—in nature, in pictures, and in the objects around them. This book can be used to help children learn more about colors. You can help them understand that color is an attribute that can be used to describe many different things: "The bananas are yellow, the fire truck is yellow, and the fish is yellow, too." Young children can also learn that a particular color does not always look exactly the same: "The red in the dancer's dress has more blue in it than the red in the flowers." You can point out that colors blend into each other and that the colors in this book are in the same order as those of the rainbow— red, orange, yellow, green, blue, purple. Children are also interested in new color names, such as turquoise, magenta, crimson, and avocado, and words to describe variations in color, such as dull, bright, warm, and cool.

You can provide children with opportunities to explore and experiment with color. Encourage them to look for all the objects of one color in the house, yard, or on a walk. Provide experiences with the way colors are formed by having the child combine drops of food coloring in water, mix paints of different colors, or hold pieces of colored cellophane to the light in different combinations.

# About Hawaii

# The islands

The Hawaiian Islands are the tops of huge mountains that began to rise from the bottom of the ocean long ago when volcanoes formed. Cracks opened in the floor of the Pacific Ocean and lava (boiling liquid rock) spurted up from the center of the earth. As more eruptions occurred the lava built up and mountains formed under the sea. The mountains became taller and taller as the lava continued to flow down their sides. Eventually, the mountains rose above the surface of the ocean.

Over time the mountains changed. Rain carved canyons into the land and made streams and waterfalls. The bottoms of the mountains were washed by waves and battered by storms, forming steep cliffs (*pali* in Hawaiian) and turning the lava into soil. After many years plants, animals, and people could live on the islands.

All of the Hawaiian Islands were formed from volcanoes, but some of the islands, including Kauai, Oahu, Lanai, and Molokai, are very old and no longer have any volcanoes that erupt. Maui is a newer island and has one volcano that seems to be sleeping. It has not erupted for a long time and no one knows if it ever will again. The island of

Hawaii is the newest island, and it is still growing as new land is added by flowing lava. The island has two volcanoes that shoot fountains of red, hot lava into the air. It is sometimes possible to get close enough to watch the fiery fountains and the moving lava. Layers of lava build up gradually, one on top of another, so that Hawaiian volcanoes slope gently and are rounded instead of forming sharp pointed cones like volcanoes in other places in the world.

# Plants and animals

For a long time there was very little life on the islands. Then plants and animals found their way across miles and miles of ocean. The first plant seeds came on the trunks and branches of trees, on wind and water currents, and were carried by seabirds.

Before the first people came there were several hundred kinds of flowering plants and ferns growing on the islands. More plants were brought by the first Hawaiians for food, medicine, clothing, and for making mats and canoes. Food plants included coconuts, bananas, yams, breadfruit, sugarcane, and taro (a purple root similar to a potato). Later settlers brought other plants they wanted for their use. New plants grew well in Hawaii's mild climate, sometimes becoming useful additions and sometimes crowding out the plants that were already there.

In Hawaii today there are many kinds of plants. At sea level there are tropical plants—orchids, anthurium, hibiscus, ginger, bananas, mangos, and flowering trees. High on the mountain slopes plants that grow in cooler climates can be found, and on the tops of the highest mountains there are some plants that grow only in Hawaii.

Insects and other small animals came to the islands the way the first plants came, carried by wind and waves. Before the first people came there were many kinds of birds and insects and even bats, but there were no frogs, lizards, snakes, or large land animals. In their canoes the first settlers brought chickens, pigs, dogs, and, as stowaways, rats and lizards. Later visitors brought many more animals, including goats, sheep, cattle, horses, cats, donkeys, deer, rabbits, frogs, and small weasellike animals called mongooses.

In addition to birds and animals that live

on land, there are many kinds of sea animals in Hawaii. Many colorful fish can be seen in the reefs around the islands. Ocean fish, such as sharks, and large marine mammals, such as whales, dolphins, and seals, also live in Hawaiian waters. Seashells can be found in tide pools, hiding among ocean rocks, and on the beaches. Shells in Hawaii are larger and more colorful than those in other islands in the Pacific.

Sea snakes, turtles, octopus, squid, crabs, shrimps, lobsters, sea urchins, and coral are also found in the ocean around Hawaii. Coral is formed as tiny animals take lime out of the seawater and deposit it around themselves to form a skeleton that builds into reefs. The reefs then join and surround the islands. Coral slowly breaks down over time and turns into the sand found on Hawaii's white beaches. Some beaches have black sand formed from lava rock.

Because Hawaii is so far away from other land, the animals and plants that reached the islands found few enemies when they arrived. With warm weather, plenty of rain, and safety, many were able to grow strong in their new home. Soon the islands were filled with plants and animals. As they adjusted to seashore, lava rock, mountain top, and *pali,* they changed. Some of them changed so much that they became different from any other plants and animals in the world — spiders that jump, snails that live in trees (and are said in Hawaiian legend to sing), ferns as large as trees, insects that cannot fly, raspberries without thorns, birds with long curved bills, and the *nene,* a kind of goose that walks on cooled lava but cannot swim.

# People

The first people to settle in Hawaii came in large canoes from a group of islands in the South Pacific. These first settlers were very brave to travel far from their homes when they were not sure that they would find land. They had no compasses to help them navigate, but they were very good at following the paths of birds and fish, the currents of the ocean and the winds, and they knew how to use the stars as guides.

The first Hawaiians were very skilled at fishing, weaving, and making canoes. They used plants, fish, and shells for making nets, ropes, bowls, fishhooks, and beautiful decorated cloth called *kapa*.

Families were important to the Hawaiians, and they especially loved children. They knew that people needed plants and animals to live and so they respected and took good care of the land and the ocean. They created songs, dances, and stories to express their feelings about the world around them and their relationship to it.

Long after the first Hawaiians arrived, sailors came to Hawaii from England. When they returned to their country they told about the beautiful islands they had visited. Soon people came from many places to visit and to live in Hawaii. People settled in Hawaii for many different reasons; to start churches and schools, to teach their religions, to hunt whales, and to start businesses. Growing and selling sugarcane and pineapple became important work in Hawaii. Groups of workers came from China, then Portugal, Japan, and later Korea and the Philippines to work in the sugarcane and pineapple fields.

Each group of people who came to live in Hawaii brought with them their language, food, dress, art, music, and celebrations. Some of these have remained the same and some have changed. People borrowed from one another, blending what they brought to Hawaii with what others, including the Hawaiians, had brought. This sharing has created a very special and unique island way of life.

Children in Hawaii today live with their families, play with their friends, and go to school just like children everywhere. They often go to the beach and splash in the waves and dig in the sand. They can play outside all year long because it is never cold, although sometimes it is rainy. Children also fly kites, climb trees, read books, and watch television. Many of them have dogs, cats, fish, birds, and mice for pets.

Children in Hawaii enjoy special foods — shave ice (cones of grated ice, flavored with sweet, colored syrup), saimin (long noodles in broth with green onions and fishcake), teriyaki (Japanese style meat marinated in soy sauce and barbecued), manapua (Chinese steamed buns), and poi (a Hawaiian food made from pounded taro and sometimes eaten with the fingers). They also eat lots of rice, fish, pineapple,

mango, and papaya, as well as hamburgers, spaghetti, salad, ice cream, and other foods that children on the mainland eat.

Families follow customs that came to Hawaii from different countries. They take their shoes off at the front door of the house the way people in Japan do; like the Hawaiians, they greet visitors or celebrate a special day with garlands of flowers called *lei*s; they celebrate New Year's Eve with fireworks the way the Chinese do, and with Japanese rice cake called *mochi*. Many families in Hawaii also celebrate Chinese New Year and two Japanese holidays especially for children, Boys' Day and Girls' Day. In schools children celebrate May Day with songs and dances of the islands and flower leis, and they observe holidays honoring Hawaiian royalty. Other holidays are celebrated the same way they are on the mainland: trick-or-treating for Halloween, decorating a tree and giving presents for Christmas, eating turkey on Thanksgiving, and giving special cards and gifts on Valentine's Day.

Mothers and fathers in Hawaii work in stores, schools, offices, and restaurants like parents everywhere. They do all kinds of jobs. They are firefighters, doctors, police officers, fishermen, teachers, lawyers, cooks, and lifeguards. Some have jobs in hotels, restaurants, and stores that are for the visitors who come to Hawaii from all over the world. Families in Hawaii today love their children very much, just as the first Hawaiians did. Together they enjoy Hawaii's beautiful beaches and mountains, and they still take time to look at the rainbows.

# More information

### HULA
The traditional dance of the Hawaiian Islands, uses hand and body motion and facial expression to interpret the rhythmic dance chants. It expresses an inner spirit and is danced to honor the Hawaiian gods, to teach about important people and events, and for entertainment.

### HIBISCUS
The hibiscus is the state flower of Hawaii. Many varieties can be found in gardens and growing wild.

### KAMEHAMEHA DAY
A rider and his horse are at the June parade that honors Kamehameha, the great king who united the Hawaiian Islands.

### ANTHURIUM
The part of the plant that looks like a flower is really the leaf, the flower is the white stem. Anthurium, originally from South America, are grown commercially on the island of Hawaii.

**MANAPUA**
Manapua are Chinese steamed buns
stuffed with pork or black beans.

**POLYNESIAN VOYAGING CANOE**
This boat is a modern version of the
double-hulled canoe used by the Polynesians in their first trips to Hawaii.

**KUMU HULA**
A highly respected person who is master of
the dance and tradition of the hula and
shares this knowledge with others.

**EPISCOPAL MITER**
Slender, pointed, orange and white shells,
which grow up to six inches in length, are
found in the sand and reefs of the Hawaiian
Islands. They stun their prey with a poison-
ous sting.

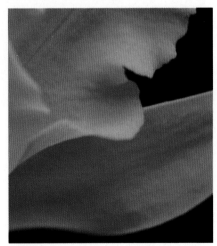

**ORCHID**
Orchids come in many forms and colors,
are plentiful in the islands, and are often
used in making leis.

**BANANA**
This popular island fruit was brought by the Polynesian settlers and is grown extensively in Hawaii.

**YELLOW TANG**
A small, yellow fish that has a white spot at the scalpellike spine at the base of the tail is a member of the surgeon fish family. The Hawaiian yellow tang is the most brilliant yellow of the species, common in the South Pacific.

**COCONUT**
The long narrow leaves of the coconut palm *(lau niu)* were used by Polynesians to weave baskets, mats, purses, hats, and other items.

**ANOLE LIZARD**
Slender, green, insect-eating lizards are found in many gardens in Hawaii. They are not chameleons though they can change their color from green to brown, tan, and grey in response to temperature and other conditions.

**BREADFRUIT**
Another food plant brought to Hawaii by the first Polynesian settlers is breadfruit. It may be eaten baked, boiled, or steamed.

**CARP STREAMERS** *(Koi Nobori)*
These colorful paper or cloth streamers are fashioned in the form of the carp, which is admired by the Japanese for its strength, perseverence, and long life. They are flown by families in Hawaii to celebrate the Japanese holiday Boys' Day, on May 5th.

**PA'U RIDER**
Women on horseback representing the different islands are a special feature of parades in Hawaii. *Pa'u* refers to the woman's skirt, a long rectangular strip of fabric wrapped around the body from the waist down. This tradition was adopted from royal Hawaiian women, who wore the *pa'u* while riding horseback.

## GLORY BUSH
This plant, with brilliant purple flowers, originally brought to Hawaii as a garden plant now grows wild at high elevations. It can be seen at Kokee on Kauai and in the Volcanoes National Park area on the island of Hawaii.

## CARP *(Koi)*
Originally bred in Japan as a decorative fish and brought to Hawaii by Japanese settlers. Large and beautifully marked carp are valuable and highly prized.

## LION DANCE
As part of the Chinese New Year celebration, dancers in lion costume move to the beat of drums to chase away bad spirits and make way for a prosperous new year.

## BIRD OF PARADISE
This plant originally from South Africa is related to the banana. The unusual flower, found in many Hawaiian gardens, is often used in decorative arrangements.

## MANGO
The sweet, juicy, orange fruit grows on a very tall tree and is eaten raw or used in pies, jams, and chutney. Mangoes originally came from India.

## LUAU
A traditional Hawaiian feast that usually includes pig and fish baked in an underground oven, taro leaves cooked in coconut cream (called *luau*), poi, and other Hawaiian foods.

# The book's creators

**Author:** Stephanie Feeney is associate professor of education at the University of Hawaii at Manoa, where she has taught since 1972 and developed the early childhood teacher education program. She received her education at UCLA, Harvard University, and Claremont Graduate School. She writes and consults extensively in the field of early childhood education and is author of two books, an introductory text *Who Am I in the Lives of Children?* and *A is for Aloha.*

**Photographer:** Jeff Reese has lived in and photographed Hawaii for fifteen years. This book represents his professional debut as a photographer. His previous credits include being a finalist in *Honolulu* magazine photo contest and having his photographs selected for exhibit at Honolulu City Hall. Educated at the University of Colorado and the University of Hawaii, he is a guidance counselor with the U.S. Army.

**Designer:** Jill Chen Loui is a freelance graphic designer in Honolulu. She was trained in art at Vassar College, University of Florida, and in Florence, Italy. She has been a graphic designer in Hawaii since 1977 and was art director for *Honolulu* magazine from 1978 to 1983. She has won a number of awards for excellence in design.

# Acknowledgments

First, and most important, we acknowledge the contributions of Eva Moravcik. This book could not have happened without her ideas, assistance, encouragement, and support. It is her spirit that shines through these pages.

We thank the Bank of Honolulu, especially Alvin Wong, manager of the Manoa Branch, for faith in us and assistance in this project.

We are very grateful to all the subjects of these photographs, children and adults; the parents who allowed us to use their children's pictures; and the preschool teachers and directors who were so helpful. Special thanks to the staff and children of Rainbow School, Jackie Dudock and the staff and children of the Valley Montessori School, Winnie Ching and Joshua Ching-Pickett, Mary, Tom, and Isaac Goya, Nancy Fargo and Christopher Fargo-Masuda, Bob, Vickie, and Michael Marks, Shair Nielsen and Kona Moon Nielsen-Yokoyama, Susie Seui and her children, Alice and Annie Ziegler, Halau Mohala Ilima (Kumu Hula Mapuana deSilva), Hula Halau 'O Kamuela (Kumu Hula Paleka Mattos), Na Hula 'O La'i Kealoha (Kumu Hula Elaine Kaopuiki).

We also thank the following for their assistance: Marguerite Ashford (Bishop Museum), Elizabeth Ayson and Stephen Quirk, Haunani Bernardino, Bessie's Lei Stand, Hale Manu Craft (Hilo), High Performance Kites, Island Manapua Factory, Puanani Mills, Moanalua Gardens Foundation (Prince Lot Hula Festival, 1984), Bruce Ushijima (Ushijima Nigishigoi), and Honolulu Fire Department, Waikiki Station.